Dear Reader,

Thank you for picking up my newest book, Dog on It. This is not my normal type of book. This is the first book that I have ever given an animal a point of view. Bernard is a St. Bernard puppy who helps to solve the mystery in this cozy romantic mystery.

I hope you enjoy reading it as much as I enjoyed writing it.

Warmly,
Rhonda

Dog On It

Rhonda Gibson

Copyright
Dog on It! © 2023
Rhonda Gibson

All rights reserved. No part of this publication may be reproduced or transmitted in any form or by any means without permission of the publisher.

All scripture quotes are from the King James Version of the Bible.

This book is a work of fiction. Names, characters, places, and incidents are either products of the authors imagination or used fictitiously. Any similarity to actual people, organizations, and/or events is purely coincidental.

Cover images by: Stacy Baron

Dedication

James Gibson, you hold my heart and encourage my writing. You have since the beginning, Thank you my love.

To my readers who were willing to read something just a little different from me. You make my heart sing with your words of praise. Thank you.

Most importantly, I want to thank my Lord and Savior. Without You I can do nothing, with You, all things are possible. Thank you!

Prologue

Bernard watched as the two angels arrived to take Mama to her heavenly home. Their spiritual bodies came right through the ceiling. He'd seen angels before but not these angels.

Mama had known that they would come for her when she breathed her last breath. She was always quoting scriptures and she'd said that the one about the angels coming to get people when they died was found in the Bible, in the book of Luke, chapter sixteen and verse twenty-two. Since he was a dog, he'd not been able to read it for himself. But she could.

He remembered her soft voice as she read, *"And it came to pass, that the beggar died, and was carried by the **angels** into Abraham's bosom: the rich man also died and was buried;"* Bernard had no idea why Mama thought there would be two but she did and that's how many God sent.

Her spirit rose from her body to meet with the angels. Even though, Bernard knew humans couldn't hear his thoughts like other dogs he couldn't help but ask, "Mama, what do I do now?"

She turned and looked down at him. Her soft smile warmed his heart. Mama knelt in front of him,

"Hannah will come and live with you. She's my granddaughter and Hannah loves puppies. I know she will love you so much."

In the six months of living with mama she'd never answered him like this. Oh, she'd seemed to understand him at times, and she always took care of him. He'd communicated with his eyes and body language but never had she ever answered a direct thought.

She smiled sweetly at him. "Do you remember where I hid my will?"

He nodded his massive head still amazed that she'd heard him.

"Good boy. Make sure the children find it before it's too late."

"I will Mama." Tears filled his eyes as he realized Mama would be gone and he'd not see her again. "I will miss you."

She stroked his head. "I know you will." As she scratched behind his ear, Mama smiled. "I always knew you understood me. You are a smart dog, Bernard."

One of the angels interrupted. "Sally."

She turned her head and looked up at the angel.

"It is time to go, you have an appointment with the Lord God Almighty."

Mama stood. "I am ready."

Bernard watched as Mama and the angels floated upwards. Mama turned one last time and said, "don't forget to help them."

He whispered, "I won't." Then Bernard laid down on the rug beside his Mama's bed where her now empty body rested.

Chapter One

October 15, 2021

A week later, Bernard still missed Mama. But she had told him the truth when she'd said Hannah would take care of him. Hannah and her brother Brody were meeting now with Mama's lawyer about the will.

Bernard shook his head. He didn't understand his new masters. Oh, he understood their words, but they seemed to dislike each other and that was what he didn't understand. He loved his brothers and sisters. Until Mama had come and taken him from the farm, they had laughed, played, and shared everything. But Hannah and Brody were not like puppies.

He liked his new friend, Hannah. She had arrived at the house first; Bernard knew she lived in town and had come every afternoon to check on Mama. Now that Mama had gone to heaven, Hannah took care of Bernard just as Mama had said she would.

The sound of her car pulling up the gravel drive made his heart leap with joy. She had returned. Bernard stretched his body and pretended he hadn't been worried she wouldn't be back.

Hannah drove a red car with shinny wheels. The desire to chase and bite them nagged at him every time he watched her leave. But Hannah always made sure he was safe in the house and could only watch her leave from the window.

***

Autumn leaves crunched under the tires as she pulled into the driveway and stopped in front of the house. Hannah sighed. She'd been listening to Brody's multiple questions ever since they had left the lawyer's office.

She got out of the car. "I don't know why she did it, Brody." Hannah filled her lungs with cool air. Normally Fall was her favorite season of the year. She loved the cooler air, hot chocolate and fluffy blankets.

Brody got out of the car too. He shut his door and stared at the house. Today he wore a nice jacket with a tie. Normally as a history teacher slash P.E teacher her brother wore sweat pants and tee shirts, she liked this more cleaned up look.

Hannah hurried to the door to let Bernard out of the house to do his business. She closed the screen as the eight-month-old St. Bernard puppy rushed past her. He ran around the house to the back yard.

Hannah rejoined Brody. She leaned against the car and looked toward their Grams house. "It's somewhere in there, Brody. We have to find it or we won't know who inherits the house."

Bernard ambled over to Hannah and sat down in front of her. He stuck his nose in the air and looked at her.

Hannah rubbed his ears. "It could be anywhere in there."

Brody gave a bitter laugh. "Do you think the old woman hide it just to force us to clean up the place?"

A smiled in remembrance of her grandmother touched her sad face. "No, I think she hide it so we would have to spend time together looking for it."

"What? Are you crazy? This house is three stories, has an attic with two wings and more cubbyholes than an antique desk. Then there is the basement, the various screened in porches and all the filled to the brim walk-in closets. Not your everyday bedroom closets, Hannah. Big closets, some of them would make nice bedrooms. We'll need all summer to shift through all the junk she has in that house. I don't have the time." Brody started to walk to his car that was parked under the apple tree.

Hannah laughed. "Fine by me, the letter that the lawyer gave us said *we* have to find the will. If one of us finds it, when the other isn't present all property goes to whoever finds it. But if we find it together, one of us gets the house and the rest we are to split. If we don't find it, there is a second will giving everything to the state, except Bernard. He's mine."

Brody groaned. "I know what the letter says."

She pushed away from the car. "I think I'll take my vacation time and stay here at Grams house until I find the will." Hannah walked to the porch and sat down in one of the old wooden rocking chairs.

Bernard hurried to follow her.

Hannah watched Brody. Would he join her or drive back to the city? She watched his shoulders slump and then he came up the old steps.

"I guess instead of going out to Mason's ranch, I'll take my fall break and extra leave time to dig through the mess." He admitted.

Hannah gently rocked. Surprise and bitterness filled her voice, "Mason moved back from the city?" Her ex-boyfriend had moved to the city shortly after marrying four years ago. He'd kept his ranch, but everyone knew he relied on a manager to keep the place running.

Brody nodded his head. He sat down in the matching rocker. "How long did the lawyer say we have to find it?"

Hannah sighed. "One month from today." Sadness filled her voice and tears her eyes. "Thanksgiving won't be the same this year without Gram."

Brody ignored her comment about Thanksgiving. He whistled low. "That doesn't give us much time. This old house is huge, and we don't have a clue where to begin."

Chapter Two

Bernard laid his head on Hannah's lap. She stroked his ears and around his collar. He knew where the will was hidden, but he didn't know how Hannah would find it. For some odd reason, she didn't pay attention to him like Mama used too.

He looked over at Brody. Hannah's brother didn't look sad that Mama had moved to heaven. Bernard knew it was up to him to help Hannah find the will. Bernard also knew he came with the house and Brody didn't seem to like him.

As if he sensed, Bernard's thoughts Brody looked down at him. "I don't suppose she mentioned what part of the house the will might be in."

Bernard looked more closely into the man's eyes. Maybe he did see sadness there. But was the sadness because Mama was gone or because he thought he had to search the whole house for the will.

"No, she did not."

"I don't understand why she felt the need to play games with her will. Grams was never a mean-spirited person." He rubbed his hand over his face.

"No, she wasn't. I think she hoped it would draw us closer to each other."

Bernard held his breath as Hannah fingered the barrel that hung from his collar. Grams had thought it would be cute to use the small whiskey barrel as a name tag for him.

Brody's sorrow filled gaze moved to Hannah. "I didn't put this rift between us, Hannah. You did."

Confusion filled Bernard. What did Brody mean by that? He looked to Hannah.

She stopped rubbing him behind his ear and pulled the letter out of her shoulder bag. "Here is the letter from Grams, if you want to read it."

Bernard noticed she didn't comment on what Brody had said about it being Hannah's fault they were at odds. His Mama or Grams as they called her, had confided in him that when Brody, Hannah and Mason were younger they were all the best of friends. Hannah and Mason were supposed to get married but then for some reason he broke the engagement and Hannah's heart. Brody had decided to remain Mason's friend and the two siblings had all but stopped talking to each other. Mama had been very sad, Hannah was right in thinking she hid the will so that the brother and sister would be close again.

He took the letter. "Mind if I take it with me? I need to get back to the city and pack, if I'm going to spend a month here."

"No, you take it. I'll see you soon."

He tucked the letter into the back pocket of his jeans. "You'll see me tomorrow. The sooner we find the will, the sooner this will be over." Brody took the stairs two at a time.

Bernard looked up at Hannah. A tear slid down her cheek as she watched her brother leave. He stood and put his paws in her lap.

She hugged him close and whispered. "Oh Bernard, if only Mason and Brody hadn't stopped loving me."

Even though he knew she couldn't hear his thoughts, Bernard asked her. "What happened Hannah?"

She gently shoved him back and got up and went into the house. Being a dog was hard when people wouldn't learn their language. He wanted to follow but she'd shut the screen behind her, forgetting that he was outside.

Bernard walked to the back fence. His two friends were waiting for him. He hadn't seen them since Mama had died.

Sheba and Babs stood in fallen leaves. More lined the bottom of the fence between them. Sheba was the oldest of the two dogs. Her coat was black, white, and grey. Her mama named her Sheba because when she was a puppy, she became the Queen in their house. A tiny dog with a big title. Babs told Bernard the other day that Sheba weighed less than five pounds when they went to see their special doctor and get poked.

Babs was a Goldendoodle who looked more like a medium sized Golden Retriever. Her daddy named her Babs because he's a big Batman fan and likes

Barbara Gordon, Batman's girlfriend at least that's what Babs thinks. Babs is short for Barbara.

Sheba and Babs were both older than Bernard and they liked to baby him. Sheba said in her calm voice, "we've missed you. How is your mama doing?"

Unaware of the sorrow their friends' words had caused Bernard, Babs took off in pursuit of a butterfly.

Bernard lowered his head; he didn't want Sheba to see the tears in his eyes. He knew mama was in a better place, but he missed her something fierce.

After a moment he heard her sigh. "The angels came to get her, didn't they?"

Babs returned. "Took who?"

He looked up and nodded. "Mama."

"I'm sorry, Bernard." Sheba nudged her small nose through the fence to offer him comfort.

He laid down in the grass and touched her nose with his. Babs flopped down on the ground too. She reached a paw through the fence and tapped his. "I'm sorry, too."

Babs hardly ever stopped moving, so it meant a lot to Bernard that his friend slowed down to show her support.

He moved his nose back and looked at his friends. "Thank you both."

Babs looked over Bernard's shoulder. "I wondered why there were new cars at your house. Was that Hannah and her brother?"

Bernard nodded. "He just left to pack to come back and look for the will."

"Our Mama told Daddy it was a shame what happened to all those kids." Babs got up and took off after a squirrel who got too close.

Bernard looked to Sheba. "Did your Mama say what happened?"

Sheba nodded. "Hannah was supposed to marry that boy, Mason. But, then he up and married a girl named Lisa. According to Mama it broke Hannah's heart real bad because Mason never said why he was breaking off the engagement just that he couldn't marry her. Daddy asked what happened after that and Mama said he up and married that Lisa girl. They had a baby seven months later. Brody and Mason remained friends and Hannah felt betrayed by both of them."

"Oh, my Mama didn't tell me all that, just part of it." Bernard felt bad for Hannah. "Brody told Hannah a few minutes ago that it was her fault that they weren't close anymore."

Babs paused long enough to say. "That's cause Hannah made him choose between her and his best friend." She continued her race around their yard.

Bernard sighed. "People sure do stupid things."

Sheba stood slowly. "Yes, especially when their hearts are broken. You better get back to the house, Hannah is looking for you." She turned and walked back to her own home.

Babs leaped over the old gal and raced her back.

Bernard sniffed around the fence. Hannah hadn't called to him, so he figured he had time to investigate the smells. The scent of rabbit twitched his nose. He followed the smell until it went past his side of the fence. Then the fragrance of squirrel tickled his snot. He followed it back the way he'd come.

"Here boy!" Hannah called from the back porch. "Time to come in for supper."

He liked the sound of that and trotted across the yard to his new Mama.

Chapter Three

The next morning Bernard woke to the sound of Hannah digging through a drawer. He now slept on the rug in her bedroom. Stretching and yawning he glanced to the window, the light outside had barely come on. Mama never woke this early; he laid back down on his rug.

Hannah scooped everything out of the dresser drawer. She laid it in the chair that sat in the corner.

Bernard didn't know why Hannah chose this room. There wasn't nearly as much stuff in it as the other rooms. Mama had used it for spare clothes and a few books. He yawned again.

He must have caught Hannah's attention because she said, "Why did Gram have to be such a hoarder?"

Bernard wasn't sure what a hoarder was, but he felt sure Mama wasn't one. Hannah had said the word like it was yucky. And Mama wasn't yucky.

"Let's go eat breakfast, Bernard and then we are going to go buy some boxes to start packing this stuff into."

He looked at the clothes she'd placed on the chair. "You don't like all Mama's clothes?" Aware she wasn't going to answer, he followed her.

They followed the narrow path to the kitchen. This path was lined with perfect piles of old and new newspapers. Mama had once told him that she'd been saving them for over fifty years. Next, they went into the kitchen. He loved the kitchen best of all. It was full of empty bowls of all sizes and egg cartons.

"Oh Grams, I wish you were here so that I could fuss at you for keeping so many cool whip bowls." Hannah looked about the room. "I bet there are hundreds of bowls lining these counters."

Bernard remembered Hannah telling Mama she needed to get rid of her bowls, she'd called them trash, but Mama had insisted they were still useful.

She opened the fridge and looked inside. "I need to clean this out too." Hannah closed the door.

Bernard looked to his empty bowl.

"Come on boy, we're going to town for breakfast." Hannah started back down the narrow hallway. "I'll get my purse and keys."

He followed. Did she say we are going to town? He'd never gone to town before. Excitement filled him. Then he slowed down. Sheba and Babs hated going to town. They always ended up at the place where they cut all their hair off or the place where they poked them. Neither of them liked going to town. Maybe Hannah was going to take him to one of those places.

Bernard stopped. He tilted his head to the side and listened.

Hannah's keys jiggled. "Come on, Bernard. I'll get you a sausage biscuit, too."

He liked sausage and biscuits. His stomach rumbled. Should he take the chance or hide? His tummy growled louder at the thought of warm sausage. Bernard swallowed hard and then followed Hannah out the front door.

She walked to her car and opened the passenger door. "Come on boy."

Bernard had only ridden in a car once and that was the day Mama had brought him home with her from the farm where he'd been born. He'd been too small to see out the window, but he was bigger now. He did as she bid and jumped into the front seat.

She rubbed his head between her hands and smiled at him as a reward for doing as she'd asked. "Good boy." Then she clipped a leash onto his collar before shutting his door.

Hannah walked around the car and slipped into the driver's seat. She looked over at him. "You don't get car sick, do you?" Concern laced her pretty features.

He had no idea. Bernard looked out the side window.

"I'll row down the window, if you get sick, stick your head out." Hannah laughed as she started the car. "Look at me talking to you, like you understand. If I keep this up, I'll be as crazy as gram was."

Bernard frowned and gave her a stern look. Mama was not crazy.

Clearly, she got the message because Hannah reached over and rubbed his head. "Not that she was really crazy, she just sounded that way sometimes." Hannah put the car into gear and began the drive to town.

He watched out the window as trees and telephone poles passed by. A field with large black and white animals in it caught his attention and he barked at the big animals. Bernard knew they were cows and wanted to say hello but soon realized they were going too fast for them to understand him.

Riding in a car was both fun and a little scary. Hannah seemed to love the wind blowing in her hair as she'd rolled down the windows, even the one above his head.

Then she did something really strange. Hannah turned on the radio and started screeching the song at the top of her lungs. She smiled at him happily.

Mama was a hummer. She listened to the music all the time. This sounded a little more fast beat then Mama's music. Hannah continued to drive and caterwaul. She reached across and playfully patted his head then began with the screaming the words again. Bernard decided it was a competition to see which of them could sing the best and joined in.

It didn't take long, and she turned the music off and said, "Alright, you win. I turned it off."

Bernard realized he should have let her win because now she frowned as they left the country and entered what he could only believe was what she had called town. The car slowed as she drove.

"You know, I should probably get some big black trash bags. We can clean the house as we search." She looked to him with sadness in her big blue eyes.

What did she mean clean the house? Mama's house wasn't dirty. It was full but she knew where everything was or went. He looked out the window. Would Hannah take away all of Mama's things?

She drove into a place where other cars were lined up as if waiting for something. When they stopped, a voice asked. "What can I get you this morning?"

Bernard looked about. Everyone was in their cars and not paying much attention to them. So, who had spoken?

Hannah answered. "I'd like two sausage biscuits, two hashbrowns and a large ice coffee with no liquid sugar and seven Splenda."

The voice repeated what Hannah had ordered and then told them to drive to the second window. He didn't like this. He didn't like this at all. Where had the voice come from? Bernard whined.

"It's okay boy. We'll be eating in just a few minutes." Hannah put the car in gear and did as the voice said.

When they came to a stop a woman opened a window. Heavenly smells drifted into the car. Bernard paid no attention to what Hannah and the woman said, he just wanted to get inside where the smell of sausage came from.

Hannah shoved him back. "Bernard, sit."

He would have laughed if he hadn't been slobbering so much. Bernard tried to push his head out her window and get to the food that he knew they were keeping inside that window.

She pushed him back again. "Get on your side and stay." This time she forced him back into his seat. The look on her face said he'd best do as she said.

Hannah turned back to the woman. "I'm sorry about that." She handed the woman money.

Bernard laid down and put his head on his paws. He was almost too big for the seat.

"He sure is a pretty boy." The woman offered with the brown sack she handed Hannah.

"Thank you. I inherited him from my Gram." Hannah kept the bag away from Bernard and took the cup of coffee.

"Well, if you ever decide to get rid of him, come see me. I'd love to have him."

Hannah looked to Bernard. Sadness still filled her eyes.

Would she get rid of him? He'd not thought that she would but did seeing him make her realize how much she missed her Gram? A sick feeling entered his stomach. Bernard no longer cared what was in the bag, only what Hannah's answer was going to be.

Chapter Four

Hannah set her coffee in the cup holder. "I'm keeping the big brute for now but will keep you in mind if I have to let him go."

She pulled the car back into traffic. Hannah smiled as Bernard sat up and looked around. "I don't know if you can understand me, Grams always thought you could."

Bernard leaned toward her. He put his big head on her shoulder.

She gave him a gentle shove. "Stay on your side."

As if he understood her, Bernard looked out the window once more. She couldn't understand him, but Hannah felt certain he understood her.

Hannah decided to focus on her driving instead of whether or not the dog understood her. She decided to take him to her favorite park. It was also a dog park. Hannah had eaten her lunch here often and thought Bernard would enjoy the park too. She pulled the car to a stop by the duck pond. Picnic tables and barbeque pits were close by. There was also a fenced in area where people took their dogs to play.

She gathered up the bag and coffee, slung her purse over her shoulder and got out of the car. Hannah walked around the car aware that Bernard watched her every move. Grams swore he was one of the smartest dogs she'd ever owned. Hannah opened his door. "Stay."

Hannah could tell that everything in him wanted to leap from the car, chase the ducks and play with the other dogs. She knew he'd be able to get past her and do just that but Bernard proved to be an obedient dog and sat still while she scooped up the lease and said, "Come on baby."

Bernard jumped from the car. Excitement raced through his body. They were going to play with the ducks and other dogs. He started for the pond only to be stopped with a sudden tug of the leash that Hannah held securely.

"No ducks!" she commanded. "Come on."

Bernard looked back longingly at the ducks as he allowed Hannah to pull him toward a table that sat to one side. She praised him for being a good boy. There was no doubt in her mind that he could have pulled away from her and gone duck chasing.

She sat the bag and coffee on the tabletop. Then Hannah looped her purse over her head so that it crossed her body. Next, she tied his leash around her waist. She could tell by his brown eyes that he'd never been tied to a person before and wasn't sure he liked the arrangement.

Hannah laughed. "Your eyes are so expressive, Bernard. I did this," she pointed at the lease around her waist, "so that my hands are free, but you aren't. It's for your protection."

She bent down and rubbed his ears. "Stop worrying so much." Then she stood. "Let's eat. I'm starving."

Bernard promptly stood up while she sat down at the table. He placed his front paws on the table.

Hannah laughed. "Don't make a habit of that." She pointed at his feet on the table and then unwrapped his sausage biscuit and pulled his hashbrown from the wrappers. "What do we do before we eat?"

He lowered his head and put his nose between his paws. Bernard waited for her to pray. Hannah couldn't resist. She took her cell phone out and snapped several pictures. He chanced a glance at her and saw that she was pointing her phone at him. Hannah laughed, his expression said, this wasn't picture time, this was prayer time. He growled deep in his throat and then lowered his head once more.

She chuckled softly and then bowed her own head and prayed. "Thank you Lord for this food we are about to eat. Amen."

Bernard raised his head and waited until she lay his food in front of him. When her hands were clear of the meal, he began to eat. He looked at her biscuit with its one little bite out of it.

"Didn't Grams teach you not to gobble your food?" she asked, after a sip of coffee.

"That's a neat trick."

Hannah recognized the man's voice. She turned to face him. "What are you doing here, Mason?"

"Walking with my daughter." He raised the hand of a cute little girl beside him. He nodded toward Bernard. "Will he bite?"

"Only if I tell him to." Hannah turned her back on Mason and resumed eating. The bread stuck in her throat. She grabbed the coffee wondering what Mason was doing here at the park.

"Well, I don't think you are going to especially since I have a defenseless child with me." Mason approached the table and sat down across from her. He scooped the little girl up and set her in his lap. "Sunshine, this is Hannah. She's uncle Brody's sister."

Sunshine smiled brightly at Hannah and Bernard. Hannah had to admit that Sunshine was beautiful. Although she looked nothing like Mason. Her hair was blonde and long with ringlets that surrounded her little heart shaped face. Grass green eyes danced with merriment. "Hi."

"Hello, Sunshine. Is Sunshine your real name or a nickname?" Hannah asked.

Mason answered. "It's her real name."

Hannah looked to him. He hadn't changed over the last three years. His dark brown hair was still unruly and his sapphire blue eyes still caused her heart to quicken. She forced herself to ask. "Why did you name her Sunshine?"

"Do you really want to know, Hannah?" Mason asked.

Hannah swallowed hard and nodded. "I wouldn't have asked if I didn't want to know." She hated that he'd had a child with another woman. A child she'd hoped to have by now and didn't but she couldn't stop wanting to know more about the little girl.

He inhaled and then slowly released the air. "The last thing Lisa said before she died was 'take care of my little Sunshine.'"

"Oh, I'm sorry." Hannah felt the heat rise in her.

He looked away. "It's okay. You didn't know. Anyway, Brody sent me to find you."

"Why? Is something wrong?" Hannah felt sick. She passed the remainder of her breakfast to ward Bernard.

He ate it even faster than his own, just in case she changed her mind. Then he dropped back onto all four legs, it was more comfortable then standing on two.

"Actually, there is. Brody had an accident last night. He called me this morning when he couldn't get a hold of you." Mason reached out to take Hannah's hand.

Hannah jerked her hand from his and demanded, "What kind of accident?" She looked at her phone and realized that it must have been on silent. Brody had called her twice and she'd missed both calls.

Mason chuckled. "It seems your clumsy brother fell out of the bathtub last night and broke his ankle. He's getting a new cast right now."

"It's not funny." Hannah protested. She stood up. "I'm going to the hospital." She was angry at herself for not being there for her brother when he'd called and Mason for taking the situation so lightly.

"Brody said not to worry about him. He'd meet you out at Grams this afternoon. Honestly, Hannah he didn't seem that hurt to me." Mason stood also and placed Sunshine on the ground.

The little girl immediately ran for Bernard. Her ponytail bounced and her green eyes flashed happily. She giggled and gave him a big hug around the neck.

He gave a tiny yelp, and she released him. Bernard wasn't taking the chance that she might choke him again and moved closer to Hannah.

Mason grabbed Sunshine's hand. "Besides, you can't take the dog to the hospital." He reminded her.

"You could take him." Hannah suggested. She hated asking him for anything but wanted to make sure Brody was alright.

He shook his head. "Nope. I promised Brody I'd keep you away from the hospital and we always keep our promises." Mason picked up Sunshine. "Don't we, Sunny?"

She nodded and giggled when he tickled her tummy.

Hannah couldn't keep the bitterness from her voice as she said. "Oh, I know all about how you and Brody keep promises." She turned and marched back to the car, dragging Bernard along beside her.

"Hannah!" Mason called after her.

The old hurt and anger tore through her leaving a new fresh gash on her emotions. She wanted to cry but didn't want Mason to see her do so. Hannah called over her shoulder. "Go to the hospital Mason and tell my brother I got the message." She stopped walking and spun around. "And while you're at it, tell him I'm going to find the will and then you two can stay out of my life."

Bernard hurried to keep up. Hannah jerked the door open. She unleased the dog, waited for him to get inside and then slammed the door shut with his leash dangling about her waist.

A few minutes later, they were speeding back to the house. Anger seeped from her like a bad odor. Why were they always keeping things from her? That wasn't fair. Hannah told herself to calm down. Brody had tried to call and Mason had gone out of his way to find her in town. Had he gone to Grams first? She slowed down and glanced at Bernard. He had laid down and tucked his nose between his paws.

Hannah stopped at a red light. She reached across and patted Bernard's big head. "I'm sorry. I'm not upset with you, big boy."

The light changed colors and Hannah focused on driving once more. Would Brody be able to help in searching for the will? Gram's house was pretty tight. Would he be able to maneuver through all her paths?

Chapter Five

When they arrived home, Hannah let him out of the car and stomped into the house. It was as if she'd forgotten all about him. How was he going to help her find the will if she continued to forget about him?

Bernard trotted around to the back of the house and looked toward the fence for his friends. There was no sign of Sheba or Babs.

A cool breeze ruffled the fur at his neck. He looked into the sky. The clouds were fluffy and white, the sun shone through them creating a false sense of summer warmth.

The breeze blew a leaf from the tree. Bernard chased it about the yard until he grew bored with the activity. His gaze moved to the house.

Hannah had forgotten to get the big boxes to put stuff in that she'd mentioned earlier. Did that mean she wouldn't be going through Mama's stuff today after all?

He laid down on the porch and soon fell asleep. Bernard dreamed of chasing ducks and a little girl who hugged too tightly.

The sound of a truck coming up the drive woke him up. He raised his head and watched as the man named, Mason got out of the truck and then hurried around to the other side to open the passenger door.

Brody slid off the seat.

He had a big white thing on his foot, Bernard tried to remember what Mason had called it earlier. Maybe he should go check it out. Bernard stood and stretched, then hurried off the porch to see what the two men were doing and saying.

Mason held two funny sticks out to Brody to take.

Brody slid them under his arms. "I don't know if I'll ever get used to these crutches." He grumbled.

Mason pulled a small suitcase from the back of the truck. "If I know you, you won't be on them long enough to get used to them."

Bernard wondered where Sunshine was. He didn't see her in the truck. He barked a hello and stood up on his hind legs trying to see through the windows.

Mason patted his head. "She's not in there ole boy. I dropped her off at home for a nap."

Hannah stepped out on the porch. She looked at her brother and then at Mason. "Thanks for bringing him out."

"It was my pleasure." Mason followed behind Brody as he swung his body on the crutches and made his way toward the front porch.

Mason asked. "Can you make it up the steps?"

Brody grunted. "I'm going to try."

Bernard watched as the two men got Brody onto the porch. Hannah held the door open for them to enter. He slipped in behind Mason before Hannah could close the door again.

"Wow, Sis. You've been busy."

Bernard looked about the room. Hannah had cleaned off the couch and chair. She'd also widened the space by pushing stuff further against the walls.

Hannah's face flushed red. "Well, I figured if you were on crutches, you'd need more space to walk and a place to sit down in each room."

Mason chuckled. "Not to mention, she cleans when she's angry."

"Oh, that's right. I'd forgotten." Brody nodded. He wobbled sideways.

Hannah huffed. "Sit down before you fall down." She guided him to the nearest chair.

Bernard watched them with interest. It was the first time he'd seen all three of them in the same room. He sensed the tension, and it made him nervous.

***

Hannah put a cushion behind Brody's back. "How does that feel?"

"Better, thank you." Her brother offered her a sheepish grin.

He was up to something. Hannah had a feeling she knew what but decided to wait them out and see if her instincts were correct.

Mason shifted from one booted foot to the other. Then asked. "Do you know which room Brody will be staying in?"

Hannah avoided looking at him. "That's up to Brody."

"Anywhere is fine. I'm hoping we won't be staying long."

"We?" Hannah asked.

Brody sighed. "You and me."

Relief washed over her. She'd been afraid Mason was going to stay too. It would be just like Brody to ask his best friend to stay and help them find the will.

She looked to Mason.

He held Brody's suitcase. "I'll put this in the first bedroom I come across." Mason pivoted on his boot heel and left the room.

Hannah turned her attention back onto Brody. "Have you given any thoughts on where we should look first?"

"Well, with this leg like it is, I thought maybe you can go get drawers or boxes that you'd like me to look through. So I guess you can start wherever you want." Brody plucked at an invisible thread on his pants.

"Let me get this straight, you want me to bring you what you need to look through to find the will." That would mean a lot of running back and forth for her.

"Well, it's either that or Mason can." Brody kept his gaze lowered.

Hannah sighed. So that was Brody's plan. Let Mason help them. She'd figured as much but then thought maybe she'd been wrong. "Does Mason know you plan on running him ragged?"

"He'd mentioned it." Mason had walked up behind her and heard them.

She turned slowly. "And I suppose you agreed?"

He tucked his hands in his back pockets and rocked on the heels of his boots. "Yep."

"Do I get a say in it?" She looked from Brody to Mason.

Mason sighed. "I told you she wouldn't like it."

Hannah wanted to scream. The last thing she wanted was to work side by side with Mason McIntosh to find her grandmother's will.

"Sure, you do. But before you say no to his helping, remember we have less than a month after today to find the will. I won't be much use." Brody pointed at his cast.

Mason laid his hand on her shoulder. "Let me help, Hannah."

She moved out from under his hand. "Why do you want to?" This was the first time in over four years that they'd even been in the same room together and now he was offering to be with her everyday until they found the will. Hannah wanted to know why.

"Because you need me."

Hannah wanted to tell him she needed him four years ago when he'd walked out of her life. But, she didn't. He was right. If they were to find the will, they needed his help.

"We do need him, Hannah." Brody's eye lids were shutting as the medication he'd taken earlier for took effect.

She looked to Mason. He was watching her with an odd expression. "Fine, but it looks like your helper is going to sleep on you."

He grinned. She'd missed that lopsided smile. His blue eyes danced with triumph. "I'll start tomorrow." He opened the screen door. "If he's not able to help, we'll do it together."

Hannah watched as he walked to his truck. She'd just agreed to allow Mason back into her life.

Chapter Six

Bernard wanted to help them so bad. He knew where the will was but none of the people in the house would listen to him or take his hints.

Maybe Hannah will listen now, he thought as he worked his way through the maze in the house. She was in the kitchen cleaning. He heard her mutter, "Maybe Grams hid it in the flour bin or the sugar bin."

He hurried into the room. Shaking his head at her. Mama wouldn't have hidden it in food. Bernard bumped Hannah's legs to get her attention.

"Hey Bernard, do you want outside?"

No, he sat down and looked up at her. Bernard lifted his head high.

She glanced in the direction of his water and food dishes. "You have plenty of food and water." Hannah returned to looking in the plastic butter dishes that Mama saved, just in case she needed them.

Bernard noticed she had gone through one large stack. A big black bag was hooked to one of the cabinet drawers and she was putting the bowls in them as she went through them. He whined. If Mama knew what Hannah was doing, she'd be upset.

Mason walked into the kitchen. "Sounds like he needs to go outside."

"I asked him, and he sat down. I'm taking that as a no answer." She didn't bother looking up at Mason.

Mason knelt beside Bernard. "Want me to go out with you?" He asked. Again, Bernard raised his head high but didn't budge.

"You're right. He's not wanting to go out." He looked to what she was doing. "Are you going to throw those away?"

"No, I'm taking them to the shelter where we will fill them with food and give them out to the homeless or anyone who comes by needing a meal."

He leaned a hip on the counter. "That's a great idea. Do you need help in here?"

"No, I'm going to go through the egg cartons next."

Mason sighed. "We've been doing this for a week, now. Do you really think she hid it in the kitchen? I mean there is a whole house for us to search and the kitchen doesn't seem like a likely place to hide a will."

Hannah shrugged. "I don't know what Grams was thinking. She might of hide it in here thinking I'd find it while going through these empty containers. I told her over and over to get rid of them. Maybe she knew I'd do that after she was gone."

"Maybe but wouldn't she be risking that you'd throw it out?" Mason ran a hand over his face.

Bernard had a feeling they weren't talking about what was really on his mind. He tilted his head and searched their faces. Over the past week, he'd observed that they both secretly looked at each other with funny expressions on their faces. It was a cross between pleasure and pain. Once more, Bernard shook his head. People were so weird.

***

Hannah hated to admit it but she agreed with him. She watched as Bernard left the kitchen. The dog was constantly under their feet. If she didn't know better, Hannah would have thought the dog was trying to tell them something.

"You're probably right. We've searched her bedroom, the office and the library. Where do you suggest we look next?"

Brody hobbled into the kitchen. "How about Braums?"

They looked at him in surprise.

Brody chuckled. "Come on you two, I'm hungry."

"Very funny, Brody." Hannah grinned to take the sting out of her words.

Mason pushed away from the counter. "I'm hungry, too. And before you suggest another sandwich from the fridge, I'm going to side with Brody and suggest we go to Braums."

Hannah's stomach chose that moment to growl. She nodded. "Alright, but we aren't going to doddle. Time is passing fast."

Brody nodded. "True but if I starve to death while looking, what good will the will do me?"

Hannah slapped him with a dish rag. "Stop being so dramatic and head out to the car. I'll get my purse and meet you two clowns outside."

Mason laughed. "I'll go find Bernard and see if I can get him to go out before we leave."

"Make sure the gate is closed to the back yard, I don't want him wandering off." Hannah instructed as they filed out of the kitchen.

A hour later, they were in Mason's truck headed back from town. Hannah hated how the two of them ganged up on her and insisted the truck would be easier on Brody's ankle.

Hannah sat between them. She found herself bumping against Mason more than she liked as he sped down the dirt road.

Brody leaned into her. "Maybe we should check the den next. Grams spent a lot of time in there."

Mason nodded. "I'm surprised that wasn't the first place we looked."

Hannah swallowed hard; she fought tears as she bowed her head to avoid their gazes. She'd been avoiding the den. Grams spent most of her time in there, reading, looking at old family photos, watching television and most recently, napping. Fond memories of Gram flooded her and she had avoided the room, knowing her grandmother would never be there again.

Brody sighed. "I've been avoiding it. Her not being there to greet us will confirm that she is really gone."

Hannah reached over and squeezed his hand. She shared an understanding look with him before releasing his hand.

They had avoided talking about the reason they'd been estranged over the last few years but talking about Gram, the will and their everyday lives had brought them closer.

They had much in common. They both were teachers. Gram had instigated that when they were both in high school. Hannah loved being a Kindergarten teacher and she knew Brody felt the same way about teaching Physical Education. They both were still single. Hannah because of her love for Mason and Brody because his wife had died last year in a car wreck. Neither wanted to find new love, it was too painful.

Although Hannah had to admit she'd never gotten over Mason. Even though he had betrayed her, she still loved him.

She chanced a glance at his profile. "Maybe we can all three do it together. It will be quicker, like jerking a bandage off a wound quicker."

Mason nodded. "I'm sorry. I know this is hard on you both. If you want, I'll look in there and you can do other rooms." He continued to watch the road in front of them as he drove.

Hannah looked to Brody who shook his head. Like her, he knew they needed to face that room and the loss of their grandmother together.

"That's sweet, Mason but we should do it. We'll have to face that room sometime, might as well be today."

He pulled into the yard. Once stopped he turned to Hannah. "If you're sure, I don't mind doing it for you."

Compassion laced his eyes. Hannah wished it were love she saw there not sympathy. "I'm sure," she answered.

Brody managed to get out of the truck and take his crutches from Mason. Assured Mason was going to help him up the porch stairs, Hannah went in search of Bernard.

The big dog laid by the back fence. Hannah could see the neighbor's dogs had joined him. She called, "Bernard! We're back."

Hannah enjoyed the crisp air. She thought Bernard would come running but instead he stayed where he was. Deciding he was perfectly fine there, Hannah returned to the house.

Both Brody and Mason had already gone to the den. Hannah took a deep breath, prayed that she wouldn't break down in front of them and then forced herself to enter her Grams favorite room in the house.

Brody sat on the little plush loveseat. Mason stood beside him, he looked as uncomfortable as she felt. The fragrance of honeysuckle filled the room. Grams favorite perfume. Tears pricked the backs of Hannah's eyes.

The room looked the same. Her focus went to the corner where Gram's chair sat in a corner. On one side of it was a ceiling to floor bookshelf filled with all manner of books, on the other side of the chair was a half size dresser a lamp sat on top of two books and together the three items created a cozy reading nook.

On the opposite side of the room was a large fireplace, a table, and two chairs. An unfinished puzzle rested on the table as if waiting for Grams to return and finish it. The television sat on the mantle. The loveseat and writing desk faced the door where Hannah now stood.

Hannah moved to the table and looked down at the puzzle. It was a tree with brightly colored birds. Grams always did enjoy watching the birds. She looked up.

Brody met her watery eyes. "Mason and I can start with the writing desk, if you want to look in the bookshelf."

Hannah didn't trust her voice. She nodded instead of speaking and walked to the bookshelf. The books on the top five shelves hadn't been touched in years. Dust covered the wood.

Gram's house might have been full of useless items but it was clean for the most part. The remaining shelves had been dusted, not even a fingerprint could be spotted on them. If Hannah hadn't taken her ladder, Gram's would have tired to climb it and clean those shelves.

Guilt ate at her. She should have taken the time to come over and dust those top shelves. Every summer she came and spent a few weeks with Gram cleaning the house in places that Gram's couldn't reach, like the top of this bookshelf. But this year instead of cleaning Hannah had taken a few college courses to get a pay increase at the school.

Brody caught her attention. He held up a doctor's bill. "Hannah, why didn't Grams tell us she was this sick?"

Hannah shook her head. "I don't know."

"This one is from the Cardiologist." Brody laid it down on a pile of papers he'd already sorted through. "From the looks of these if the stroke hadn't taken her, her heart might have."

She pulled down a book and ruffled through its pages. A slip of paper fell out, but it was nothing more than a faded grocery receipt. "They said she died in her sleep. For that I'm grateful."

"Me too."

Hannah spent the rest of the afternoon going through all manner of books. What impressed Hannah the most was that there was a whole row of Bibles, one of commentaries and another of various Bible study books her grandmother had done or started over the years. Those had been in the center of the bookshelf and then it had turned to Gram's favorite cookbooks and various craft books. When she got to the bottom Hannah sighed in frustration. No will.

Brody and Mason had moved to other parts of the house. The writing desk had proved to be void of the will as well. Brody had muttered something about checking to see what other desks there were in the house. Mason said he'd check upstairs, since stairs weren't easy for Brody to climb.

Hannah left the den to check on Bernard.

Chapter Seven

Bernard lay on the back stoop absorbing the last rays of sun. He lifted his head when Hannah sat down beside him and in a tired voice said. "Hey boy, mind if I join you?"

He sat up to make more room for her.

She surprised him by wrapping her arms around his neck and sinking her face into his fur. He leaned into her to offer whatever comfort she seemed to need. Her fingers brushed the barrel around his neck.

Hannah turned her head so that her cheek still rested against his neck. "We have searched all the obvious places and can't find the will." She said softly, tearfully.

Bernard shifted his weight slightly. He knew where the will was. If Hannah knew how close she was to finding it, Bernard realized Hannah would be so happy. But how could he tell her? He'd tried showing her but she just didn't understand.

Hannah pulled away from him. "Are you ready to go in and eat?" She stood, not waiting for a response.

Since the backdoor was locked, Hannah led the way around the house. Mason was just coming out the front door. Bernard wondered how the two would act.

They confused him with the way they responded to each other. Sometimes they were nice and polite, other times Hannah gave him the cold shoulder. She was never outright rude but even a dog could tell Hannah didn't want Mason around her. Especially when they were alone, like this.

"I'm heading out. I'm not sure if I'll be back tomorrow. Mom says Sunshine is running a fever." He tucked his hands in his back pockets.

Bernard looked up at Hannah. Concern lined her face. "I hope she will be okay."

"Me too. She's had ear infections in the past. That might be what this is." He didn't leave.

Bernard wondered why he didn't leave. He was just a dog, but he was concerned about Sunshine. Shouldn't her father be hurrying off now? Or was he more interested in spending time with Hannah?

***

Hannah was thinking the same thing. "If Sunshine were my daughter, I'd take tomorrow off." She said the words aloud and immediately regretted them.

Mason sighed. Sadness filled his voice, "I wish she was our child." Then he walked away, leaving Hannah feeling speechless.

What did he mean by that? Was he trying to tell her he regretted the past and having a child with someone else? Or was she reading more into his words?

Hannah held the door open for Bernard then walked into the house behind him. Brody sat in his spot beside the door.

"Hannah, I've had a crazy idea."

She raised her eyebrows at him. Had he overheard her and Mason's conversation just now? "What?"

"Now hear me out before you say no." He waited for her agreement.

Hannah nodded. She walked to the loveseat that sat across from him and waited.

"Well, we know the will is at this house, right?"

"Right."

He scooted up on the edge of his chair. "How about we create a scavenger hunt?"

Brody reminded her of long-gone days when they were kids and he'd come up with a new game to get them into trouble.

"What kind of scavenger hunt?" Weariness laced her voice.

"Something simple."

She eyed him for a moment. "I like simple."

"And, I'll let you do all the planning. That way, you will know I am behaving myself."

Hannah liked that too. If her brother wasn't doing anything but letting her plan and helping where she needed him, it might not be a bad idea.

They could make it like a fall festival day for her teacher friends. A day to get out and have fun. "Let me grab a notebook." Excitement filled her voice. What if this worked? With the added help, they could find the will and move on with their lives.

She went to her Grams writing desk and pulled out several sheets of honeysuckle stationary. It wasn't the notebook she was looking for but Grams really didn't have notebooks. Like everything else, unless she or Brody introduced her to new technology, Grams had always gone old school.

Hannah took the paper and hurried back to Brody.

"I hope you don't mind but I ordered delivery pizza. I'm starved."

Hannah laughed and sat back down. She grabbed a big gardening book off the end table and pulled her legs under her so she could plan out the scavenger hunt event. "You keep eating out and you are going to weigh a ton by the time that cast comes off."

"Naw, I have the metabolism of a teenage boy." Brody patted his flat stomach and grinned.

"And the appetite to match." Hannah teased back. She looked up at her brother. These were the times she'd missed over the past four years. Times of fun and teasing.

"I think I'll invite all the teachers from my school, that's sixteen."

"Is that enough people for a three-story house with an attic and a basement?" Brody hobbled to the window and looked out.

"If you are looking for the pizza, you have about an hour wait. And to answer your question, yes, I think so. Grams hasn't been to the attic or basement in years." She tapped the pencil against her chin.

"Really? An hour? Why so long?" Brody dropped back into his seat.

Hannah shook her head. He grew up here too. For a grown man he often times could be such a drama mama. "You know why, stop being such a baby." She didn't think he'd appreciate being called a drama mama. Hannah hid her grin behind her paper.

She lowered the paper. "I need an incentive to get them to come. Maybe I could offer to do playground duty for the rest of the year to the lucky person who finds the will." Hannah heard Brody's snort. "What would you offer them?"

Bernard circled the rug and flopped down.

"Money." Brody answered. "Everyone loves money."

Chapter Eight

She shook her head. "No, I think playground duty replacement for a year would make them happy."

"Sis, I'm not sure that will be enough to get them to come out here and look for a will that they may or may not find." Brody crossed his arms over his chest.

Hannah agreed. She sat for several long minutes trying to figure out how to get the teachers to take a Saturday and come out.

Brody grinned. "You know, we could make it into an event like a fall festival."

"I don't know. That's a lot more work."

As if he didn't hear her, Brody continued. "Write this down. We could have a cake walk, that way everyone has a chance at taking a cake or cupcakes home. Maybe we could have a Halloween Parade and whoever has the best costume would win a prize. Or maybe…"

Hannah interrupted him. "Hold on." She looked at him sternly. "Who's going to bake all those cakes or cupcakes?"

He shrugged. "We can buy them."

"You are going to buy sixteen to twenty cakes?"

He nodded. "Sure. I can do that."

Hannah frowned. "Well, a cake walk can't be our only activity. She wrote down Brody's idea of a cake walk and costume party. She looked back up. "And what's the prize for the best costume?"

"Twenty-five dollars."

"This is getting costly for you." Hannah commented as she wrote down twenty-five dollars beside the words Halloween Costume Competition.

Crunching of tires coming up the drive had Brody hobbling back to the window. "Finally," he muttered as he picked up the money for the pizza and continued to the door.

The smell of warm pizza filled the room. Hannah's stomach growled. She set her pen and paper down and went to help Brody.

She took the pizza and the two-liter pop from the driver while Brody paid. Hannah's mind continued thinking about the Fall Festival. She set the pizza on the table. If they were going to have events for the people, she could leave scavenger clues for them to find with the last one being the will in the house.

Brody closed the door and sat back down. He opened the box and sighed. "This is awesome."

"I'll get cups of ice." She placed the pop on the table and hurried to the kitchen.

Bernard stayed behind with Brody. Hannah watched the dog get into his praying position and grinned. She prayed that pizza didn't upset doggy tummies.

As she re-entered the room, she asked. "Do you think Mason would donate a few bales of hay for our event?"

Around a big mouth full of food, Brody answered. "I'll ask. What are you going to do with them?"

She handed him his glass and sat back down. "I was thinking we could use a few to make a pumpkin bowling game. And place a few about the yard for people to sit on. That kind of thing." Hannah jotted those ideas down, then set the paper aside so she could eat.

Brody nodded. "I'm sure if we give them back when we're done, he won't mind at all."

They ate for a few minutes in silence.

Hannah thought about Mason. He hadn't changed much at all over the past four years. She admired the way he checked up on Sunshine throughout the day. He'd turned into a good father, not that she'd ever doubted him. "I wonder how Sunshine is doing?"

Brody swallowed. "He texted a little while ago and said her fever was normal by the time he got home."

"That's good." Hannah yawned. It was still early but she was ready for a hot shower and bed. "I'm going to take a shower and then I'll clean up this mess." She announced as she stood.

***

Bernard watched her pick up the papers and pen then leave the room. He looked to Brody who waited until Hannah had left the room and been gone a couple of minutes before standing up and following her.

Bernard followed.

Brody stopped and listened until he heard the water running in the bathroom. Then he hurried back to his phone in the living room.

This wasn't right. Bernard didn't like this at all. Was it his imagination or was Brody walking on his hurt foot like it didn't hurt?

Brody dropped into his chair and pressed some buttons. Bernard tilted his head and listened. He was rewarded with the sound of Mason's voice in Brody's phone.

As soon as Mason said hello, Brody asked. "How's Sunshine doing?"

"I texted you a little while ago and said she's fine. Her fever went down when I got home."

Brody grinned. "I'm glad to hear that. I have a favor to ask."

Mason's warm chuckle filled the lines. "Just one?"

Brody shrugged. "For now."

"What can I do for you?" Mason asked, his voice sounded hesitant as if he wasn't sure he wanted to do whatever it was Brody was going to ask.

"Hannah's planning a fall festival so that we can incorporate a scavenger hunt for the will. I was wondering if you'd mind supplying a few hay bales."

"How many is a few?"

Brody closed the pizza box. "I'm not sure yet. Hannah is still working out the details."

"Whose idea was this?" Mason asked.

"I suggested the Scavenger Hunt and she's taken it and ran. Sounds like she's going to come up with a lot of fun." Brody took a drink from his glass and then grinned. "If we play our cards right, our guests will find the will for us."

Bernard waiting to hear what Mason had to say about that. But the line was quiet.

"You still there?" Brody asked.

"Yeah, do you know when she plans on having this fall festival?"

"Not yet but I would imagine it will be right before Halloween because she's planning a costume contest."

Mason's voice sounded filled with concern. "So probably next weekend. That's fast. I hope she doesn't bite off more than she can chew."

"It's Hannah. She's the most organized planner I know. I'm sure it will be great." Brody put the lid back on the pop. "So are you coming tomorrow?"

"If Sunshine is feeling alright, I don't see why not."

"You could always bring her with you."

Mason's voice changed from concerned too hesitant. "I don't know, Brody. Hannah might get upset."

"Look, if you want her to like your daughter, you are going to have to let them spend time together."

Brody sighed. He walked to the wall and listened. "I have to go, Hannah is out of the shower. I'm going to surprise her and carry our dinner back to the kitchen."

"Night." Mason said before hanging up.

Bernard looked to Brody. Hannah's brother seemed tricky. He'd called Mason when she wasn't there to talk about her and he didn't seem to have any trouble walking when she wasn't about. He sniffed at Brody's cast.

"Watch out Bernard." Brody had picked up the pizza box and the bottle of pop and was doing as he'd told Mason and carrying them into the kitchen.

Bernard stepped back. He left Brody and went to find Hannah. Surely, she'd be back in her room and dressed. He used his nose to push the door open. Hannah sat on the bed, with the pillow behind her back and was looking at the pages of paper.

She smiled at him and indicated the papers in her hand. "This might work, Bernard."

He walked to the edge of the bed and laid his head on her leg. Bernard liked the feel of her pj's, they were soft and smelled like a warm summer day.

"Sis?" Brody tapped lightly on her partially opened door.

"I'm coming." She started to get off her bed when his voice stopped her.

"No need to clean up. I did it for you."

Bernard looked to Hannah's shocked face. "Thank you."

"Night." And then he was gone.

She put her leg back up on the bed and patted Bernard's head. "You know, there may be hope for him yet."

Bernard looked to the door. He didn't know. His doggy senses told him Brody was up to something.

Chapter Nine

The next morning, Mason arrived with several square bales of hay in the bed of his truck. Hannah watched from the window as he hopped out and began unloading them.

The muscles worked under his shirt as he piled them up under the apple tree. She'd missed Mason. Memories of them working the hay meadow together flooded before her mind. She drove the truck, Mason and Brody stacked hay into the bed. Now Mason probably had a fancy baler but when they were younger, they were the balers.

A little blonde head poked out of the truck. "Can I gets out?"

He continued working but called back to her. "In a minute, Sunshine. Let me finish unloading this and then we'll head inside."

Hannah frowned. It wasn't that she disliked the little girl, but she was a reminder of why Mason had left her for another woman. Everyone whispered about Lisa and the baby, after they'd gotten married. There was no way that they could hide the fact that Lisa was pregnant before they got married. She still had a hard time believing it was true but every time she saw Sunshine, Hannah had to face reality. Mason had been unfaithful to her and had married Lisa.

"Looks like it's bring your daughter to work day." Brody said close to her ear.

Hannah jumped. "Don't sneak up on me like that?" She scolded.

"I'm not the one hiding behind curtains." Brody placed a hand on her shoulder. "It's okay to still have feeling for him."

Hannah turned to face him. "Brody, what's to stop him from hurting me again?"

"He never wanted to hurt you before." Brody dropped his hand. "I hurt you, are you ever going to forgive me?"

"You're my brother."

Brody looked over her head at Mason. "He's the man you love more deeply than yourself." Then he turned and walked back toward his bedroom.

Sadly what he said was true. Hannah knew she loved him and would never love anyone else. She looked down at Bernard. Sometimes she wished she was just a faithful dog without the cares of the world on her shoulders.

Hannah picked up her purse. "Stay with Brody, Bernard. I'll be back soon." She opened the door and stepped out into the crisp morning air.

Mason smiled when he saw her. "Good morning."

"Good morning. I see Sunshine is feeling better." Hannah nodded toward the truck where Sunshine had decided to climb out of the window to get out of the truck.

He hurried to catch her. "Yes, she is. The little monkey." Mason tickled her belly before setting her feet on the ground. He turned his attention back to Hannah. "Where are you headed this morning?"

"The library." Hannah walked the short distance to her car. "I'm going to print some flyers for the Fall Festival. Brody can tell you all about it." She started to slip inside the car.

How he covered distance so fast was a mystery to her. He hadn't run but here he was standing at the car door. "Mind if I look at your flyer?"

Hannah pulled it up on her phone and showed him.

He leaned forward and wrapped his hand around hers before pulling the phone closer to look at. "I don't have my glasses with me." He muttered.

Her hand felt warm and tingly everywhere he touched her. Just like old times. Hannah didn't bother pulling away, she knew he wouldn't hold her there long.

"You forgot something." He released her and leaned back.

Hannah turned the phone to her and studied the flyer. It was all there, cake walk, Halloween costume contest, pie eating contest, pumpkin bowling and the scavenger hunt. She looked up in confusion. "What did I forget?"

He smiled. "The hay ride. After finding the last clue on the hay ride they can venture into the house for hot chocolate and to find the last item of the scavenger hunt Sally's will."

"But, we don't have enough hay or a wagon or a place to go for the ride." She protested.

"Sure you do. You can use my hay and wagon; I'll even drive it for you. And we can take them down the road, through the corn field and then back around to your house."

Hannah shook her head. "I don't think Mrs. Shackleford will let us go through her corn field."

Mason grinned. "Leave it to me. Can you add a hayride to the flier?"

Hannah searched his handsome face. "Are you sure she'll let us?"

"I'm sure."

A smile broke across her face, "then I'll add the hayride. Thank you."

He reached out and tucked a strand of hair behind her ear. "You're welcome. You still have the most beautiful smile I've ever seen."

A squeal tore across the morning air. Hannah looked to the house and found Sunshine with a death grip on Bernard. Brody stood with them on the porch. The knowing smile put her into action, and she quickly closed the car door.

Mason stepped back and waved as she pulled out of the driveway.

Hannah glanced in her rearview mirror and saw Sunshine being caught up in Mason's arms and swung about. The joy on the child's face brought a smile to Hannah's lips.

Chapter Ten

Bernard didn't like this, not one bit at all. He road in the back of the truck with his ears flopping in the wind. He felt pretty sure Hannah wasn't going to like it either.

Mason drove, Sunshine sat in the middle and Brody beside her on the other side. They had put him in the bed of the truck and said it would be fun. He did not think this was fun.

Thankfully Mason pulled up in front of Joe's hardware store. Bernard listened as he asked Brody, "are you sure Hannah's going to be alright with this?" He held one of her flyers in his hand.

"We are just inviting a few more people out to the Fall Festival. Why wouldn't she be ok with it?" Brody answered.

Mason shrugged and went into the store. A few minutes later he returned without the flyer. "Joe was happy to post it." He said climbing back inside the truck.

Bernard had seen Brody take one of the flyers from Hannah's small pile when she'd not been looking. Then as soon as she'd left for the grocery store, Brody had told Mason they needed to go to town and make more copies to post about town.

They'd gone to the office store first and now Brody was having Mason take them into different stores and posting them.

Once more the wind blew in Bernard's ears. He hated it and laid down trying to keep his head down and his ears safe. When they stopped again, he sat back up and looked around.

This time they were in front of the barber shop. Bernard frowned as Mason left the truck again and disappeared inside.

"No!" Bernard howled after him. But, Mason didn't hear him and returned a few minutes later without another flyer.

"How many copies did you make?" Mason asked, getting back inside the truck.

Bernard heard Brody answer, "just five."

"So where to now?"

"How about the feed store?"

Mason backed the truck up and away they went again. Bernard howled his discomfort, but the wind seemed to carry his complaints away.

It was another thirty minutes before they headed back home. Mason had dropped off flyers at the flower shop and the bakery before heading home.

Bernard jumped from the truck. Brody smiled as he climbed the front steps. "Looks like we beat Hannah back."

Mason glanced at his friend. Did he suspect that Brody wasn't supposed to drop off more flyers. He held the door open for Sunshine and Bernard to follow Brody inside. "Does she know we made more flyers and posted them in town?" Mason asked, uneasily. "If not, she is going to set both of our tails on fire."

Brody put the flyer he'd taken from Hannah's pile back. "We are just ensuring that plenty of folks come to help. Hannah's teacher friends might not be able to make it on such short notice."

Sunshine seemed to ignore the grown-ups. She climbed up on the couch where Mason had placed a small box of toys. "Daddy, do you have a tail?"

Brody laughed.

"It's just a way of saying Hannah's not going to be happy, if Uncle Brody's plan backfires somehow."

"What's backfires?" Sunshine pulled a small stuffed rabbit from the box. She looked up at him with big green eyes as she hugged the toy close.

Mason smiled at her. "You know how sometimes you do stuff and grandma doesn't like it and you get in trouble?"

She nodded. "I gets in trouble."

"Well, it's something like that." He turned his gaze on Brody. I do not need to get in trouble with Hannah."

Brody smiled. "Then I wouldn't mention our little field trip."

Bernard wished he could talk. This was something he felt Hannah should know about but knew he couldn't tell her. But, he still hadn't figured out a way to tell her where the will was and knew he'd never figure out how to tell her about this.

Aggravated at both men, Bernard walked to Mason and bumped his legs. He needed to go outside and even though Mason had just done a very bad thing, Bernard knew he'd let him out the back door.

Mason looked down at him. "Want to go outside?"

Bernard yelped and raced to the back door. He prayed, Sheba and Babs would be outside, he really needed to talk to them.

Mason let Bernard out and shut the door behind him.

Bernard saw Sheba in her back yard and made a wild dash for the fence where he could talk to her. The old gal was getting a little hard hearing but turned at his call.

She came to the fence at a slow pace.

Bernard looked about for Babs but didn't see her anywhere. When Sheba joined him at the fence, he asked. "Where's Babs?"

"She stepped on something, and our Mama is taking her to the poking place."

Bernard laid down so that he'd be closer to her height. "That's too bad. I hope she's alright."

Sheba snorted. "Oh, that one is a ham. She let on her paw was killing her until someone mentioned the word Vet. Suddenly she was doing better but Mama said she wasn't taking any chances."

"I hope Babs doesn't get a poke." Bernard had been poked when he was little but not in a long time. He didn't enjoy the experience and knew Babs hated it.

"How are things going at your house? Have they found the will yet?" Sheba asked as she licked her front paw.

"No, they just don't listen to me." Bernard hated that he hadn't been able to show them where the will was hidden.

Sheba looked up at him. "Tell me, how are you telling them?"

Bernard raised his head and looked up to the sky. "Like that." He answered lowering his head again.

"What else?" She went back to licking.

Bernard had noticed that Sheba cleaned herself a lot. "I don't know what else to do."

"Well, you could try getting them to give you a bath and then you would be able to show them better." Sheba looked up at him and laughed. "I can see by your face you don't like that idea. But it might be the only way. Get messy and see what happens." She stood up slowly. "I think I heard Mama and Babs drive up. I'm going to go check on her. Just consider rolling in the dirt and letting Hannah give you a bath." Sheba turned and ran back to her house.

Bernard laid where he was. He didn't want a bath. But, if it got closer to the end of the month deadline, he'd do it. He'd hate it but he'd do it.

Chapter Eleven

"Come on, Brody. We can't stop looking just because we are having the Fall Festival." Hannah banged on her brother's bedroom door again.

"Alright, already."

Hannah looked down at Bernard. "Should we go in and pull him out of bed?"

Brody's voice came through the closed door. "I said I'm up, go away."

She patted Bernard on the head. "I don't know why he's so grumpy in the mornings."

The sound of something solid hitting the other side of the door was her reward.

Hannah grinned. "Breakfast will be ready in ten minutes, if you aren't at the table and ready to eat then, you forfeit a meal." She turned and walked back to the kitchen where the hearty aroma of an egg, sausage and cheese casserole welcomed them.

She sat down at the table and picked up her papers and pen. "I don't know what else to add."

"To what?" Brody grumped from the doorway.

Hannah didn't bother looking up at him. "The Fall Festival."

He slid into the chair across from her. "Sis, you've been working on that non-stop for three days,

I think you have it all organized and ready to implement."

"What if this doesn't work?" The timer went off on the oven. Hannah got up to pull breakfast out.

"Then we keep looking until we find it or the time runs out." Brody hobbled over to the dish drainer and pulled out two clean plates and two forks.

"You forgot the knife." Hannah said as she placed the pan on a hot plate.

He pivoted, grabbed a knife, and then limped back to the table.

"You seem to be getting around better." Hannah noted, taking the knife, and giving her brother an appraising look.

"Um, yeah, it's feeling better today." Brody sat down and held his plate out for her to serve the casserole. "Do we have any salsa?"

Hannah chuckled. "Yep, never leave home without it." She served him and then went to the fridge for the condiment he'd asked for.

Bernard watched them eat in silence. They'd forgotten grace since both of them were in their own thoughts. Mama would say to watch out, they'd have indigestion by afternoon for not giving thanks.

"Hannah, can I ask you for a favor?"

Bernard watched as she chewed slowly and nodded.

"Mason needs help deciding on which flatbed trailer to use for our hayride. He's asked if you would mind coming out to the ranch and helping him decide." Brody scooped up more casserole and waited for her answer.

Bernard looked to Hannah. She laid her fork down and picked up the papers once more. "I'm sure either will be fine."

"So, you won't go help him?" Brody made a tisking sound. "What would Gram think of that? He's trying to help you and you won't make a decision for him."

"Really, Brody it's not that big of a decision. I've invited sixteen teachers. So, the small one will do."

"What if those teachers bring their families? Mason doesn't know how many people are in their families. You do. Come on, he's not asking you on a date."

Hannah glared across at him. "I didn't say he was."

"Good. Then you'll help him decide." Brody shoved the last of his breakfast and made a quick escape.

Hannah watched. "He sure can move on that ankle when he wants to." A frown marred her features.

Bernard walked over to his bowl. What would Hannah think if she knew that when no one was around, he'd seen Brody walking around just fine? And what was she going to say when she found out her brother had invited a lot more people than she had invited?

Hannah scrapped the rest of her breakfast in his bowl. She muttered something about meddling brothers and then began cleaning off the table.

Bernard silently prayed over his breakfast. *Lord, please help Hannah and Brody find the will and Lord, be with Hannah as she helps Mason pick the best wagon. Oh, and thank you for this food.* The casserole with his dry dog food tasted wonderful. He wished he could have more but by the time he'd finished eating, Hannah was heading down the stacks of odds and ends, looking for Brody.

Three and a half hours later, Hannah was pulling onto the McIntosh Ranch. She wasn't happy about it but Brody was right, since he was helping her the least she could do was tell him which trailer would be best for their hayrides.

The ranch was just as she remembered it. Tall trees scattered over green pastures dotted the landscape. A large pond sat off to the right. Mason or his mother had taken the time to fence it in and place benches and flowers around its edges.

A lot of other things had changed as well. Cows had been moved away from the house and now filled the pastures in the distance. Hannah grinned. Mason had taken her advice four years ago and moved them further out.

Hannah remembered him telling her, if it would make her love her new home even more, he'd move them. She'd never seen it happen since he'd broken off their engagement the week after they'd talked about the cows. Her happiness quickly turned to sorrow.

She tried to ignore the changes and just get up to the house. Mason had texted Brody that he'd wait for her at the main barn.

It came into view as she rounded the curve. The big barn had been painted red and doubled in size. She immediately saw the two wagons in question. Each was harnessed to horses. The smaller one had a black mare that stomped her feet. The larger had two bay horses attached to it.

He'd been standing in the doorway watching her drive up. Mason walked to the car and smiled. "No Bernard, no Brody? I get you all to myself?"

Hannah felt her face flush. He almost sounded happy to have her alone. She pulled the door open and nodded. To take the attention off her blushing cheeks, Hannah asked. "Why are both wagons hitched up?"

"Well, they ride differently, and I thought you might like to get a feel for them before you decide which one to use." Mason rocked back and forth on the heels of his boots.

She walked to the black mare and approached slowly. The horse bobbed her head at Hannah. "You sure are a pretty girl." Hannah slowly reached out her hand and rubbed the black's nose.

Mason had followed her. "Do you remember Rolling Thunder?"

Hannah nodded. Rolling Thunder was one of Mason's father's favorite racehorses.

"That's Rolling Beauty, she's one of his daughters." He stroked the neck of one of the bay mares. "We bought him three years ago."

That would explain how the ranch had improved so much. A racehorse could make or break a beginning rancher, it looked to Hannah like Rolling Thunder had been a good investment.

She decided to change the subject back to the wagons. "I think the smaller will work better for the hayrides."

"I thought so too but Brody wanted you to see both wagons before you decided." Mason bent down and checked Rolling Beauties hoof, the one she kept stomping. He took out his pocketknife and popped a pebble out. "There that probably feels better, doesn't it little girl?"

Hannah assumed it did, since the black mare stopped pawing the ground. "Well, if that's all, I better be going." She started to walk back to her car.

"Not so fast. You haven't ridden in the wagon to see how it feels." Mason walked to the back and extended a hand to help her into the wagon.

She eyed his hand. "You're kidding, right?"

"Nope. Plus, I want to see how Beauty will do pulling it." He wiggled his fingers.

Hannah sighed. "I can get in by myself." She walked to where he stood, turned to hop on backwards but he surprised her by placing his hands around her waist and lifting her onto the bed.

"There you go. Now go find a haybale to sit on, while I climb aboard." He instructed with a grin.

"Really, Mason this isn't my first hayride." Hannah still did as he said and found a bale close to the back of the wagon as far away from the seat where Mason would be sitting.

He looked over his shoulder, grabbed the reins and asked. "Ready?"

Hannah barely had time to nod before he had Beauty trotting around the barn. It was a bumpy ride to say the least.

Mason looked back and smiled broadly. "Now move to the center and see how that feels." He slowed Beauty down to a slow walk.

Hannah did as he asked, thankful he'd slowed down. Once she was seated, they were off again at a trot. This time the ride was a little smoother. She looked to see where they were going.

Mason guided the mare to a group of apple trees. The sweet fragrance drifted on the cool air. When they were in the apple grove, he stopped. "How was that?"

"Better." She confessed with a smile. This orchard had been here for years. Hannah had started picking it's apples as a teenager. She loved it here.

"Move on up here." He patted the bale right behind him.

Hannah did as asked.

Mason turned back around and clicked his tongue to get the mare to go into a trot. Hannah hated leaving the cool, sweetness of the apple orchard. She closed her eyes enjoying the cool breeze on her face. There were so many things she loved about the ranch. With her eyes closed, she could pretend she was a teenager again and falling deeply in love with Mason.

He pulled the wagon to a stop.

Hannah opened her eyes expecting to be back at the barn. Instead, she found herself looking at the stream that ran on the east side of the orchard. "Why did you stop here?"

Mason leaned toward her.

She thought he was planning to kiss her and inched back.

A low warm chuckle built in his throat. He pulled a picnic basket from between the bales and grinned. "I hope you don't mind, but I haven't had lunch yet." He hopped off the wagon seat and tied the horse to the tree, making sure she had plenty of lead to graze about the tree.

Hannah took a deep breath, so this had been the plan all along. She didn't like being manipulated by her ex-fiancé and her brother.

Chapter Twelve

Mason had already walked to the water's edge. He was far enough away that they wouldn't get wet but close enough they could enjoy the soft gurgle of the clear water as it sloshed over the rocks. "I always thought this was a perfect place for a picnic, didn't you?" He spread the blanket that had been tucked into the basket on the ground and then placed the basket on top.

He knew she loved this spot. They'd shared their first kiss here and he'd proposed here. Hannah chose not to answer.

"Come on, you can't stay up there while I eat alone." He walked back to the wagon and extended his hand up toward her.

Hannah ignored his hand and climbed over the side of the wagon. Not very graceful but she didn't have to touch him.

Mason shrugged and walked back to the blanket and basket. He sat down and began to pull small plastic tubs from the basket. "I brought fresh strawberries, cheddar cubes, ham chucks and your favorite butter crackers."

She crossed her arms over her chest and looked down at him. "I thought this was your lunch."

He ignored her stance and continued pulling out containers. "For myself, I brought fried catfish bites, a tub of mama's coleslaw and a shiny green apple."

"What nothing to drink?"

"Hannah, darling, you know me better than that. He reached inside the basket one more time. For you, sparkling water and for me a thermos of coffee…"

She finished his sentence, "black, no sugar."

"Right." He looked up at her with big blue eyes. "Please, have lunch with me. There are a few things I need to tell you, that I should have said long ago."

Hannah wasn't sure she wanted to hear what he had to say. But, she also couldn't deny she needed to hear whatever he planned on sharing. She sat down across from him and picked up the water.

"Mind if I say a quick prayer over our meager meal?"

"No." Truth was, Hannah doubted she'd get one bite past her dry throat.

Mason bowed his head and thanked the Lord for their meal. He asked for guidance in his words with Hannah and he asked that Hannah be given an understanding heart. Then he closed with amen. For several minutes he kept his head bowed but when he looked back up at her there were tears in his eyes.

Never had she seen Mason cry. Even as a teenager, when he'd almost cut his arm off plowing the west field, he hadn't cried.

He looked across at her and said, "Hannah, I don't expect your forgiveness. I know I hurt you and I want to explain what happened four years ago."

She didn't trust her voice so simply nodded.

Mason took a deep breath and began. "I met Lisa in College. She was a good study buddy but nothing more then a friend. Lisa was an only child, a sickly child and came from a wealthy family. Her parents placed her on a pedestal that sooner or later she was bound to fall from." He stopped to see her reaction.

Hannah didn't know how to feel, so far it sounded like Lisa had everything, every little girl dreamed of.

He continued. "When we graduated, I teasingly told Lisa that when she fell, I would be there to catch her. As you know, I came home, and you and I fell in love. But Lisa also fell but not in a good way. She got pregnant but the man didn't want any part of being a father, he preferred being rich and single. When Lisa told her parents, they wanted her to get an abortion, but she refused. Her parents turned their back on her. If that wasn't bad enough, cancer was discovered in her cervix area and had spread to her bones."

Hannah was horrified. How could Lisa's parents demand she abort her child and then turn their back on her.

She listened closely as Mason pressed on. He was like a man who held pent up information and just wanted to get it out. "Lisa contacted her parents and told them about the cancer. Again, they urged her to get rid of the baby and then she could come home. Lisa refused. So, they accused her of lying about the cancer and refused to help her."

Hannah broke in. "That's when she contacted you." The words tore through her like a dull knife.

"Yes."

"Why didn't you tell me?" Tears pricked her eyes. If he had explained things to her, they might have been able to figure something out.\

"Lisa asked me not to tell anyone. She didn't want to bring shame on her parents."

"But they had cast her out." Hannah argued.

Mason nodded. "Yes, but they were still her parents. I think she thought that once she had Sunshine, her parents would love both her and the baby. If she was married when she had Sunshine, they would save face. Everyone would simply think the baby was a preemie."

Hannah sighed. "But she couldn't be treated for cancer carrying Sunshine, could she?"

"No, she couldn't. Our original plan was to marry, have the baby and when her parents took her and the baby in, I would be free. We would get an annulment and I could explain everything to you."

Hannah's heart broke for Lisa. But, she couldn't contain the anger she felt toward Mason. Did he think she would have betrayed Lisa? Was that the reason she hadn't shared this with her. He'd simply told her he couldn't marry her and walked out.

Brody had chased him down and then come home defending his actions. Brody said Mason had good reason but wouldn't share the reason with her. When you love someone, you are honest and open with them. Hannah had been left feeling like neither Mason or her brother loved her enough to be honest with her. They had hurt her real bad.

"Hannah, Lisa died shortly after giving birth to Lisa. She lost a lot of blood and her body was too weak from the cancer to fight. Her last request was that I take care of her Sunshine." His voice broke. "I wanted to tell you."

Hannah hardened her heart. "Then why didn't you? Lisa's request was that you not share her story to save her parents pride but once she was gone, Lisa wouldn't have known what you did.

Mason searched her face. "You were so hurt and angry. I wanted to give you time to heal, to forgive me."

"And you thought now was the time?" Hannah stood up and walked back to the wagon.

He followed her. "I had hoped that we could start again. The last couple of weeks we have been friends."

Hannah shook her head. "No, you were Brody's friend. You were helping him. I understand you think you were doing the right thing by Lisa, but you never considered what the right thing was for me. For us." Tears burned her eyes.

Mason returned to the blanket and untouched food. "I'll clean this up and take you back."

"No, I will walk back. That wagon will be fine for the hayride. Goodbye, Mason." Hannah's heart felt crushed. She wanted to say it was all okay, that he'd done the right thing. But, to her way of thinking he hadn't done what was right by her.

When Hannah got back to the barn, the other wagon was gone. She assumed Mason had beat her back and put it away. Hannah climbed into her car and headed back to Grams house.

Once on the road, she changed her mind. Brody would be waiting. Who knew what he expected, probably for her to come in and say all was forgiven and she and Mason were a couple again. But that wasn't so. She didn't think they would ever be again.

***

Bernard paced. Where was she? Hannah should have been back hours ago. He'd heard Brody talking to Mason and knew Hannah was upset about something.

Brody was worried too but he told Mason Hannah just needed time alone to think. She probably went back to her apartment in town.

He looked out the window and whined. Where was Hannah?

Chapter Thirteen

Bernard still sat at the window the next morning when Hannah drove up. He barked to let Brody know that she was back. Bernard didn't care where she'd went or why, he was just happy to have her home.

Brody limped out onto the porch. "Where have you been? I've been worried sick."

She stepped around him. "I don't answer to you, Brody. I haven't in years."

Bernard looked at Hannah's brother. Sadness filled his face; Hannah's words had cut deep. He didn't understand why people said such mean things to each other.

Brody followed her inside with Bernard on his heels.

The two of them stayed out of her way. Hannah said she was going to the third floor to search for the will. When it was lunch time, she came back down and acted as if nothing had changed but Bernard could feel the tension in the house.

Brody sat at the kitchen table while Hannah gathered lunchmeats, cheese, veggies, bread and condiments for them to make sandwiches. Bernard watched him, watching her.

"Are we going to talk about it, Hannah?" Brody finally asked, when she'd sat down.

"No."

He made a sandwich. "You're right, it's none of my business."

"No, it isn't." She poured them each a glass of iced tea. "Tomorrow is the scavenger hunt. I think everything is in order. I'll need to get up early, to get everything into place for our guests. Hopefully, one of them will find the will and we can both get on with our lives."

Bernard heard the bitterness and sadness in Hannah's voice. He wanted to fix whatever had happened, but he couldn't even get her to see the will. There was no way a dog could get two people who obviously loved each other to heal over past hurts and love again.

***

As she'd said, Hannah was outside setting up for the Fall Festival long before the sun came up. She had made squares out of spray paint on the grass and set up a table for the cake walk. Then she'd moved on to creating a runway made from tarps for the Halloween

Costume contest. Next, she'd moved the bales of hay to create a bowling alley with tall gourds for pins and small round pumpkins for bowling balls. As the sun came up, she walked the route of the hayride and placed items that the people could spot along the way. Lastly, she placed a banner over the door of the house and said the person to find the will was the winner.

Mason had come by the night before driving the wagon for the hayride. He'd brought Beauty and made her comfortable beside the house. Then he'd left.

Hannah returned to the kitchen and made her favorite coffee and toast. She wasn't in the mood to eat much more than that.

Brody entered the kitchen a few minutes later. He poured himself a cup of coffee. "Hannah, I'm sorry I hurt you. It was never my intention. I'd made a promise to a friend and like Mason, I felt I had to keep that promise."

She walked over to him. "Brody, you're my brother and yes I get angry with you but I will always love you, even when I don't believe you love me too."

He grabbed her and held on tight. "Hannah, love isn't something you turn on and off. I didn't stop loving you, I just couldn't break my word. Remember Papa always said a man's word is his bond."

Hannah knew Brody was telling the truth. She knew he loved her. When the tears started flowing, she couldn't stop them. Her brother rubbed her back and promised never to keep secrets from her again.

Two hours later, Hannah had showered, washed her face and dressed to meet her friends and spend a fun day laughing. She knew at some point she'd have to face Mason but not until after they found the will.

She put Bernard in the backyard. Hannah realized he'd grown even more over the past two weeks. As a large dog, he might scare some of the children and she didn't want that. He was a good, gentle dog who would more than likely be the one getting hurt, not the children if she let him run loose in the house.

The teachers began arriving right on time, as predicted by Brody some of them brought their children or grandchildren. She was glad that she'd ordered lots of cupcakes for the kids.

Mason arrived right on time as well and took on his role of Hayride engineer. He'd brought Sunshine with him who had a good time telling everyone to climb aboard sounding more like a train engineer than a hayride engineer.

Hannah watched the little girl with new eyes. Her mama was gone, and her grandparents wanted nothing to do with her. Hannah's heart went out to the little girl.

Everything was going splendidly. Hannah went inside to make hot cocoa in a large pot so that when they got back from the hayride, the adults could search for the will while the children ate cupcakes and drank cocoa.

While she worked, she heard Brody greeting people and telling them to stay on the main three floors of the house, not to go into the basement or the attic. Hannah grinned. Grams had mended the tear in the sibling's relationship.

She heard a crash upstairs. Hannah went through the paths until she got to the staircase. Two women who were not teachers were standing there. "What happened?" Hannah asked.

They looked at each other and shrugged. As she was going up, Hannah heard one of them say. "Probably one of the men broke a lamp but they can afford it. I heard Mr. Briar say that whoever finds the will gets ten thousand dollars."

Hannah turned around and looked down the stairs. She could no longer see the women. Who was Mr. Briar? And where did he get the idea, they were offering money to find the will?

She arrived in the room she thought the noise had come from only to find it empty. Hannah hurried to the next room and found the men in question. They looked to be in their sixties. One of them held a crowbar and was about to pop the paneling off the wall. The other was searching the room like a mad man and had knocked over the lamp. Thankfully it wasn't one of Grams favorites.

"What are you doing?" she demanded in her best schoolteacher voice.

He lowered the tool. Excitement filled his voice. "We think there's a hidden door behind this paneling. That's where she hid the will."

She walked across the room and jerked the crowbar from his hand. "There are no hidden doors or rooms in this house. Do not tear down the walls. You straighten up that lamp and then get out of this room." Hannah pointed to the door with the tool.

They did as they were told and then filed out of the room like two wayward children.

Hannah followed close behind. Now she could see lots of people milling through the various pathways. She didn't recognize most of them. Where had they come from and how had they known about the scavenger hunt?

Conversations were loud and ridiculous. She walked past the music teacher who was talking to her friend Bonnie, the other Kindergarten teacher. "Not only is she promising that she'll cover our playground duty for the rest of the year, but I heard she's going to half her inheritance with whoever finds the will."

"Bonnie, you know that's not true." Hannah said as she passed.

Bonnie's eyes grew wide, and she pointed behind Hannah. Hannah turned just in time to see one of Grams towers of newspaper tittering forward. It came crashing down as two teenagers ran through, shoving and pushing each other.

"Watch out!" Hannah called after them. They continued running and hitting everything in sight.

Magazines, newspapers, computer paper, mail, they were in the paper, and it was flying in all directions.

The sound of screams came from another room. Running footsteps could be heard all over the house as people raced looking for the will. Hannah barely avoided the cereal boxes as they toppled over.

"Gee Ho Sifat!" Brody yelled. More crashing came from that direction.

Hannah recognized that it was coming from her grandmother den. She raced in and found Brody standing with his mouth hanging open. The bookshelf had been pulled from the wall and books had gone everywhere. The table with the puzzle laid on its side and puzzle pieces were strewed about the room. Another woman who looked to be in her forties was jerking the cushions off the chairs. "Stop!" Hannah yelled to no avail.

A strong voice, low and powerful filled the chaos. "She said, stop."

Everyone turned to find Mason standing in the doorway. "It's time everyone go home."

Hannah walked to the fireplace and sat down on the hearth. The room was destroyed. Tears slid down her cheeks.

The woman and girls filed past her, looking shameful. It didn't fix the fact that they had ruined the only room in the house that she truly cared about. No longer could she smell honeysuckle or envision her grandmother reading by the bookshelf. Pain fresh and sharp caused the tears to flow faster.

She heard Mason clearing the house of the inhabitance. His strong no-nonsense voice had people leaving quickly. She heard the cars as they drove away but none of it mattered.

Brody had left when Mason had so Hannah was all alone in the room. Soon the house became quiet once more. She walked to the bookshelf, it rested on its side. Hannah bent over and picked up her grandmothers favorite Bible.

A bookmark fell out. She picked it up and read it.

1 Peter 4:8 And above all things have fervent charity among yourselves: for charity shall cover the multitude of sins.

Tears poured from Hannah's eyes. Grams was gone but there were still people who loved her. Mason being one of them. He'd hurt her but he'd hurt her too. Thanks to Grams bookmark, Hannah felt like the Lord was telling her to give Mason another chance and to ask him to forgive her, too. She realized not everyone would read the scripture the same way she did but that didn't matter. Hannah knew she loved Mason and loved him deeply.

"Hannah? Are you okay?" Mason stood in the doorway.

She laid the Bible down and walked to him. "I'm sorry. I was wrong, too."

He opened his arms and she walked into them. Hannah looked up at him, she needed him to tell her he loved her and she was forgiven.

Mason buried his face in her hair. "Oh Hannah, I'm the one who is sorry. I'm a foolish man who didn't handle things correctly."

She tilted her head and looked into his beautiful blue eyes. His head descended and then it happened.

Bernard ran into the room and jumped on them. Mud flew everywhere.

Sunshine followed the big dog. She too was covered from head to toe in mud. "Look Daddy, we got to play in the water." She grabbed Mason around the legs and hung on for dear life.

Brody chose that moment to run into the room too. "I'm so sorry, Hannah I had no idea things would get this out of hand. Some nincompoop turned the water on in the back yard, it's flooded."

Bernard jumped about the room, throwing mud everywhere. He race back and forth between Hannah and Sunshine giving sloppy kisses.

Hannah squealed as the dog grabbed her with his front paws around the waist, coating her with even more mud and doggy kisses her. What the dog was so happy about was beyond Hannah's comprehension. She looked to Mason who was smiling as if he'd found the will or won the lottery.

He scooped Sunshine up. "Well, this is our que to leave. This girl needs a good bath." Mason looked to his best friend, "Brody, good luck explaining all this and the fact that you can run on a broke ankle."

***

Bernard was having the time of his life. He'd managed to play in the mud, even though he didn't want a bath he knew one was coming now.

He watched as Mason carried the little girl from the room. Bernard decided then and there that Sunshine was his little girl and they were going to have many adventures together.

"Bernard, stop jumping all over the place." Hannah laughed as she grabbed his collar.

Brody stood on his broken cast. "You're not angry, Hannah?"

"No but I might get that way once you explain to me what you did and why you lied about your foot." She pulled on Bernard's collar. "Come on you two, this dog needs a bath."

Brody followed them out the door.

Bernard dug his feet into the floor and pretended he didn't understand what was going on.

"Why do I have to help bath that monster of a dog?"

Hannah stopped pulling on him. "Because I have a feeling you are responsible for the people being here who turned on the water, creating mud that now Bernard has all over him. And he isn't in the mood for a bath so it's going to take both of us to get him cleaned up."

Bernard allowed Hannah to pull him through the house. He was amazed at the mess. Mama would have been so upset if she hadn't went home with the angels. Her stuff was all over the house and not in the orderly manner she liked it.

"I'll see if I can find Grams old wash tub. I think it's in the basement." Brody offered. "Meet you outside in five minutes."

Bernard and Hannah went out the back door. Sheba and Babs stood on the other side of the fence. Babs called, "Can I come play with you? That looks fun."

He didn't bother answering her. She didn't realize a bath was in his near future although it probably wouldn't matter to her, Babs liked getting wet.

Sheba through her thoughts his way. "I see you got dirty and now will need a bath. Good for you."

"I hate baths." Bernard answered.

He was about to add more when Hannah said, "come on boy, lets take off your collar. I'm going to have to clean it up too. Look at all this mud."

She worked his collar until it hung in her hands.

Bernard sat down and waited. Would she find what he'd been hiding all along?

Hannah tilted the collar and heard the soft thud. She looked at the barrel. And read it aloud, "Bernard, nine, one, eight – four, two, six- three, one, one, two. I'll have to redo your barrel boy. Grams phone number doesn't work anymore."

Brody came around the house dragging a big wash tub. He looked at Bernard with distaste. "I can't believe how muddy he is."

"Look at this collar. It's caked with mud too." Hannah extended the wet mess to her brother.

He pushed her hand away. "I don't want that."

Something thudded in the barrel again.

Hannah looked at Bernard. "Is there something you want to tell me? Like what's in your barrel."

Bernard raised his head high, exposing his neck once more. "I tried to tell you like this." He knew she couldn't hear or understand him, but he thought it anyway.

"You don't think she'd put it in his collar, do you?" Brody asked, suddenly willing to touch the barrel.

Hannah pulled it out of his grasp. "I think so, and I'm the one who found it." She twisted the lid on the barrel, but it didn't budge.

"Well, you didn't expect it to just pop off, did you?"

"Shut up, Brody." Hannah left them standing in the yard.

"All this time and you've, had it?" Brody asked Bernard as they waited.

He beamed. "Yep."

Bernard was happy to see Hannah return. She had a pair of pliers and the barrel.

"How in the world did she get this on so tight?" Hannah asked working to get the lid off.

"No idea." Brody answered, "We may have to break it open to get out whatever is inside."

Hannah stopped twisting. "What if it's not the will?"

"We won't know what it is, if you don't get it open or let me try to open it." Brody sat down on the back step.

Hannah handed him the barrel and pliers.

Bernard watched as Brody twisted. They heard a soft pop and then he grinned. "I think I broke the seal." Then he handed it to Hannah. "Go ahead and open it, Sis. You found it."

Hannah took the barrel and titled it so that the contents would fall into her hand. An oblong ball of bubble wrap landed in her palm. She handed Brody the now empty whiskey barrel.

Bernard held his breath as she unwrapped each layer. He remembered the day Mama had put it in his barrel. "Help them to find this, Bernard. But don't let them find it too soon." He frowned; he'd forgotten that part until just now.

Hannah grinned at him. "Good boy." She then held a jump drive up for Brody to see. "We've been so stupid."

"Hey!"

She laughed, "I said we. We thought it was going to be in a folder. Grams fooled us by hiding it right under our noses."

"I sure am glad you didn't get rid of him." Brody patted Bernard's wet head. "Let's get him cleaned up and then get cleaned up ourselves. We should go out and celebrate our findings tonight."

Hannah laughed. "This might not be the will. It might be like our scavenger hunt and just be a clue to the will."

Brody's face fell. "Do you really think Grams would do that?"

She shook her head. "No, but it was fun making you think she might."

Epilogue

Thanksgiving 2022

Bernard sat beside Mason waiting for Hannah to walk down the aisle. He was the ring bearer. Sunshine the flower girl and Brody was giving away the bride. Bernard still couldn't believe he was in a wedding.

Mama would have been so proud of him. He'd helped Hannah and Brody find the will. Sunshine was now his very best friend. And he'd grown into a big boy.

The Vet had told Hannah that he now weighed one hundred and eighty pounds. She'd hugged him and said he was her big boy.

As much as Bernard loved his first Mama, Hannah's Gram, he now loved Hannah too. Just like Mama had said, Hannah took care of him.

During the last year, together they had cleaned out Gram's house. She left the house to Brody. In her will she'd left another letter saying that if all went well, Hannah would be getting married soon and wouldn't need the big old house.

She'd been right.

It took time but after almost a year, Mason asked Hannah to marry him. She'd agreed but only if she could have a Thanksgiving wedding.

The church was decorated in fall colors and bright leaves covered the tables in the other room.

They weren't real leaves, but they were just as pretty. Pumpkins were also used as decorations.

Bernard couldn't wait to sample the wedding cake. It was three tiers, and the roses were orange and yellow. Mason said it wasn't a typical wedding cake but theirs wasn't a typical wedding. After all they have a St. Bernard as the ring bearer.

He watched as Hannah and Brody came down the aisle. Music magically started playing. It wasn't the kind Hannah normally listened to and thankfully she wasn't screeching with it.

Sunshine skipped to her daddy. The orange and red flower petals jumped out of the basket. It's not the way Hannah told her to walk or toss the flower petals but she was happy so that made Bernard happy.

Hannah was beautiful. She wore a white dress and had blue and orange ribbons in her hair. Her eyes glistened and she smiled really big.

Mason wore a black suit with an orange flower. He watched Hannah walk toward him.

When they stopped in front of Mason, Brody kissed Hannah on the cheek. Then handed her to Mason. He took her hand in his and they faced each other.

Sunshine whispered real loud, "Did I do good, Mommy?"

Everyone else watching laughed. I chuckled a little too but no one can see when a dog laughs.

"You did great." Hannah assured her.

Being a dog has its ups and downs. Bernard knew he liked the ups. He wondered if he'd ever get to be a part of another mystery. This one was fun, so he hoped it wasn't his last mystery.

More From Rhonda Gibson

Wagon Train Baby (Coming May 2023)
Wagon Train Wedding
How to Write a Cozy Mystery
A Bride for Benjamin
Stuck on You (Christmas Book)
Baby on Her Doorstep

I have many more, but these are my most recently published.